BIBLICAL

PRINCIPLES

FOR

SPIRITUAL

GROWTH

In Sermonic Structure

Okino Broomfield

This book is created to help Christians worldwide to improve their spiritual lives.

ISBN: 9798848867299

Table of Contents

<u>Acknowledgment</u>

I want to thank the Lord for His grace towards me and for enabling me to complete this work. I also want to thank Him for the wonderful people that he has placed in my life to assist me with this project.

I thank three people who helped me greatly with this book; Dr. Bryan Wallace, Nickeisha Broomfield-Jones and Neisha Bryan-Broomfield.

Dr. Wallace has imparted a lot of knowledge where Homiletics is concerned so that I can structure my sermons effectively. I thank God for the dedication that he has toward his word and in return imparting his knowledge to the future generation.

Nickeisha Jones has spent countless hours transcribing, organizing, and editing for my ministry.

Neisha Broomfield for the many ideas and support for making this book a possibility.

__Introduction__

What is Spiritual Growth?

Spiritual growth involves knowing more about God and pushing towards Him. As believers, we all have a start in our journey with God. Some of us may be more familiar with the nature of God while others may be completely new to the concept of salvation. Spiritual growth can reflect our actions, and at times we might ask ourselves: Am I living out more of God or more of self?

At times, as believers, we are not doing what we should be doing to build up the body of Christ, so we keep the gospel to ourselves by keeping our mouths closed. Jesus said in **Luke 10:2**, *"The harvest is plentiful, but the labourers are few."* And so, it should be our nature to work to build up the body of Christ, seek restoration when we are lost, put our trust in Jesus, lean to His solution to our problem, know the importance of love and show that love to others, and seek greater faith and his divine protection.

If we want to grow spiritually, we need to heed to the principles of God within the Bible, ask the Holy Spirit for help and he will lead us into all truth and in the wisdom and mind of God.

Chapter 1: The Nature of Kingdom Workers

By studying the Honeybee

42 "But the Lord said to me, Tell them, Do not go up and fight because I will not be with you. You will be defeated by your enemies.

43 So I told you, but you would not listen. You rebelled against the Lord's command and in your arrogance, you marched up into the hill country.

44 The Amorites who lived in those hills came out against you; they chased you like a swarm of bees and beat you down from Seir to Hormah". (Deuteronomy 1:42-44)

Introduction

As I think about verse 44, I'm asking myself the question, why did the Lord refer to the Amorites as bees? The Bible says that when we study God's creation, we can see His truths. And so, I researched bees, and the more I learn about bees, the more amazed I am about the lessons of creation. Not only are bees astounding creatures that play an important role in our world, but we can also learn a lot from them about being better members of our families and churches.

There are many kinds of bees, about 20,000 different species! But for now, I want to especially focus on the common honeybee. I think the Lord made the honeybee for a very special purpose, more than just pollinating flowers, which helps us grow crops so we can have something to eat. I believe that He created them to give us special insight into His nature and what He wants from us. Have you ever heard the expression "busy as a bee"? There is a very good reason for that, you see, bees are some of nature's hardest workers. To make just one tablespoon of honey for your toast in the morning, a bee has to visit 4,200 flowers! A worker bee will make up to 10 trips a day, visiting 400 flowers. And to make just one pound of honey, worker bees need to visit more than 3 million flowers and travel the equivalent of three times around the world! Of course, they don't mind doing it because they care about their hive. And the harder they work the happier and more productive their colony can be.

In a bee colony, every bee has a job. There are worker bees, queen bees, and drones. The queen lays the eggs, and the workers find nectar, make honey and protect the hive with their stinger. What would you think if I told you that a bee drone doesn't have a stinger? That means they can't defend the hive, and not only that, but they also don't gather nectar, make honey, or lay eggs either. At first, drones might appear to be a little worthless! But in a hive, no one is worthless. The drones help feed the larvae, the babies, with royal jelly among other responsibilities.

This royal jelly is a milky secretion produced by worker bees. It typically contains about 60% to 70% water, 12% to 15% proteins, 10% to 16% sugar, 3% to 6% fats, and 2% to 3% vitamins, salts, and amino acids. So, they might not collect pollen or have the highest position in a beehive, but they have a vital part to play. And they give their all to do it.

Honeybees are very loyal to their queen. They will go wherever the queen goes and do whatever is needed to make sure their leader is healthy and happy, and they'll work hard to help the queen do her part for the hive, which is to lay eggs so the colony will grow. Everyone else works to feed the larvae and protect the queen. It wouldn't work very well at all if the other bees ignored or even hurt the queen, would it? It would lead to an unhealthy queen and could even destroy the entire colony!

On the other hand, bees are very optimistic. A bee will never resist a flower with nectar because of thorns, but rather go straight to the flower. Being positive also helps bees stay persistent when looking for nectar. Sometimes they must travel for miles to find a flower full of nectar. They also must deal with people shooing them away from their gardens. But have you noticed that they always come right back? They're focused on their mission of gathering sweet nectar, not the obstacles that stand in their way.

Honeybees will fly as far as eight miles in search of nectar and whenever they find what they are looking for, no matter where they find it, they will turn right around and make a "beeline" back to their hive so that all the bees can join in the good news and go get some nectar. When they get back to the hive, they start doing an amazing little dance that tells all the other bees where they found the nectar.

There are some bees out there that look a lot like honeybees but aren't. A honeybee stings only once, and then it dies. But another kind of bee called the yellow jacket can sting more than once. They also make honey like honeybees, but instead of nectar from pretty flowers, yellow jackets get nectar from dead animals! And, while honeybees live high up in the trees, yellow jackets live on the lowly ground.

You see, some people are afraid of bees because they can plant a painful stinger on your skin. But bees don't want to sting anyone! It is their very last resort because when a honeybee stings someone, the bee will die soon after. But bees are always thinking of the colony. If they believe their hive is threatened, they will throw themselves at the enemy and lay down their lives to protect the others.

A study of the community of the honeybees will help us to understand the nature of kingdom workers. (Deuteronomy 1:42-44).

Building up the Body of Christ

Just as the honeybees work to make their colony happier and more productive, as Christians, we should also work to build up the body of Christ.

One of the ways the bees build their colony is to go out in the field in search of nectar because without nectar their colony will die, and no matter where the nectar is, the bees will travel up to eight miles from their hive to find it, and when they find it, they don't keep it to them self but rather go straight back to the hive to let the others come and partake of the sweet nectar.

Likewise, as Christians, we must go out into the world in search of souls to build up the body of Christ. Jesus said to his disciples in **Matthew 9:37** that *the harvest is truly plentiful, but the laborers are few*. You see, Jesus knew that people are out in the world harassed and helpless and he described them as a sheep without a shepherd. It is not for us to keep the gospel to ourselves and say that "I am safe". When you experience Jesus, it is for you to tell somebody about this man.

When the Samaritan woman realized that she had experienced Jesus, the bible says that she dropped her water pot and ran straight to the city and said come see a man, and not just any man but a man who will reveal my secret. Brethren, it is our duty as believers to tell someone about Jesus. No matter the status that they have in life, we must meet people at their level so that we may win some for the kingdom's sake. The Apostle Paul said in **1 Corinthians 9:22** that *"To the weak I became weak, to win the weak. I have become all things to all people so that by all possible means I might save* *some"*. Let us do our duties as believers and work to build the body of Christ.

Another way the bees build their colony is for each one to fulfil their assignment. Every bee needs to fulfil its duty for the hive. And so, the queen bee must lay eggs, the worker bees go out in the field in search of nectar, while the drone bees take care of the larvae by feeding them with royal jelly and they give their all in doing it.

Whatever your assignment is, it is important to the building up of the body of Christ. And you might be asking the question: what is my assignment? But I am here to tell you today that you can find your assignment in the gifts of God. And no matter how simple you believe your gift is, there is an assignment and it is for you to do your work to the best of your ability. **1 Corinthians 12:12-14** says ***"Just as a body, though one, has many parts, but all its many parts form one body, so it is with Christ. For we were all baptized by one Spirit to form one body - whether Jews or Gentiles, slave or free - and we were all given the one Spirit to drink. Even so, the body is not composed of one part but many".***

As a member of the body of Christ, you have a role to fulfil. Part of that role is allowing God to express his graces or his gifts through you for the benefit of the church and the rest of the world. There is only one anointing and only one spirit, but there are different kinds of graces/gifts. God will choose which graces he wants to express through each member of his body. Every member has all his graces within them, but God will place us in specific offices to complete different functions, all of which are vital and important. So, no matter where God places you in the body of Christ, fulfil your assignment.

Be Optimistic

Just as the honeybees are optimistic, as Christian we should also be optimistic.

No matter what is before the bees they will never give it attention but rather put their focus on what can help their colony which is nectar, and anywhere the nectar is, even if the nectar is in a place that seems dangerous, they will always look past the danger and see the positive. It is our duty as believers to focus on the positive. **Philippians 4:8** says *"Whatever is true, whatever is noble, whatever is right, whatever is pure, whatever is lovely, whatever is admirable if anything is excellent or praiseworthy think about such things"*. Do not focus on the bad that people have to say about you, do not take the negative negatively but rather take the negative positively.

Because the devil wants to distract us from our purpose, he will use whatever is around you to bring that distraction and fear. In the book of **Matthew 14:29-31**, *"Jesus said to Peter Come!"*, then Peter got down out of the boat, walked on the water, and came toward Jesus. But the bible says that when he saw the strength of the wind, he was afraid and beginning to sink, but he cried out, *"Lord, save me!"*

Immediately Jesus reached out His hand and took hold of Peter. You see, the devil wants to replace our faith with fear for us to take our eyes off our purpose, but God said "***I have not given you a spirit of fear but of power, of love, and a sound mind"***. I want to tell you brethren that if you keep your eyes on Jesus,' no matter how the storm of life blows, it shall not move you out from your faith because Jesus is our anchor.

The hymn writer said, *"We have an anchor that keeps the soul Steadfast and sure while the billows roll, fastened to the Rock which cannot move, Grounded firm and deep in the Saviour's love."* And if by any chance you have been distracted, you can cry out like Peter and the Lord will save you because he **"can keep you from falling, and to present you faultless before the presence of his glory with exceeding joy".** and so it is our duty as a believer to stay positive in our situation.

Bees also show their optimism by staying persistent. No matter how we shoo the bees away out of our garden, they will always return because there is something that keeps them in your garden, and they will not leave until they have completed their mission which is to fill themselves with nectar to bring back to the hive. Likewise, as believers, we should stay persistent because persistence drives results. Let us not be all over the place because you ask for something and you didn't receive it and so you ask for something else, but let us keep our eyes on the prize and keep asking.

In the book of Daniel, the angel said to Daniel that from the day you have set your heart to pray, your prayer was answered but the prince of Persia have hold the answer captive. You see when you pray, at times the devil will want to steal your answer, but he can only steal your answer when you stop praying. But, Daniel, when he realized that he did not receive his answer, the bible says that he went on 21 days of fasting about his answer and when he kept on praying, there was a shift in the realm of the spirit where Michael the arch angel was released to set loose his answer that was in bondage. When you persist in prayer, the devil cannot steal your answer. When you persist in prayer, the devil must release that which was stolen from your fore parents, and when you persist in prayer, that which the Lord has in store for you will be yours.

Do not be a Counterfeit Christian

Just as the honeybees are not counterfeit, as Christian we should not be counterfeit.

The honeybees will follow the queen wherever she goes. The yellow jacket, on the other hand will never follow the honeybees queen but rather, they will try and confuse us in calling them honeybees, but the truth is that their nectar is from dead animals and they live inside of the carcass. They will even try to deceive the honeybees and try to get inside the hive to steal their honey because of the likeness in their appearance.

For one not to be a counterfeit Christian one should follow Jesus. In **Philippians 3:1-3**, the Apostle Paul contrasts true and counterfeit Christianity. But to understand that section of Philippians, you must know a bit of history. Soon after the gospel began to spread among the Gentiles, some Jewish men who claimed also to believe in Christ began teaching the Gentile converts that they could not be saved unless they also were circumcised according to the law of Moses (**Acts 15:1**). They did not deny that a person must believe in the Lord Jesus Christ, but they added to the faith in Christ in the keeping of the Jewish law, especially circumcision, as necessary for salvation.

This issue was debated and resolved in Jerusalem at a council of the church leaders where it was decided that Gentiles do not have to become Jews or be circumcised to be saved; but that every person, Jew or Gentile, is saved by grace through faith in Christ alone. You see, the devil will always add or take away from the scripture to confuse the Children of God and many times he will use earthly wisdom to break the bridge between you and God and that's how he was from the beginning. God said to Adam in the book of Genesis that *"if you eat of the tree of knowledge of good and evil thou shalt surely die"*. The devil added to that sentence and said to Eve **"thou shall not surely die"**.

Don't allow the devil to deceive you of the truth. You also have some people that the devil will steal their attention amid service and allow them to hear what he wants them to hear. I remember a story about this man that went to a church and he was there in the midst of service so distracted, and the preacher quoted from **Psalm 14:1** and said *"the fool said in his heart there is no God"* and the only part that comes home to the man is the part that says "… there is no God" and he left service spreading rumours in the community saying that pastor said there is no God. I want to tell you my friend that **the devil is like a roaring lion seeking whom he can devour**. Don't be a counterfeit Christian and listen to the voice of God because his voice makes a difference. **Jesus is the only way, the only truth, and the only life.**

For one not to be a counterfeit Christian, one should be pure in heart. **Matthew 5:8** says *"Blessed are the pure in heart, for they shall see God".* Jesus Christ teaches us that people should take care not only of their physical hearts but also their spiritual hearts. You have some people that look like Holy people and when they praise God, their mouth is the loudest in the church, but the reality is their heart is far from God. **Matthew 15:8** said that *"These people draw near to Me with their mouth and honour Me with their lips, but their heart is far from Me".*

Natural hair doesn't make a person holy. Dressing modestly doesn't make someone holy. It is the life that a person lives that will make them holy. The Bible says that *"man looks on the outward appearance, but the Lord looks at the heart"*. I want to tell you that a person can fool man but they cannot fool God because God is all-knowing and so, he is a God that knows everything about us, even more than we know of ourselves.

<u>Summary</u>

Therefore, having seen the nature of kingdom workers as shown in the study of the nature of the honeybees, we as Christians should be able to develop a life that is comparable to that of the bees.

As the honeybees work to make their colony happier and more productive, as Christians we should be workers also to build the body of Christ, and we can build the body of Christ by loving our neighbour, and we can build the body of Christ by fulfilling your assignment.

As the honeybees are optimistic, as Christians we should also be optimistic, and we can be optimistic by focusing on the positive, and we can also be optimistic by staying persistent.

As the honeybees are not counterfeit, as Christians we should not be counterfeit Christians, and one way not to be counterfeit is to follow Jesus, and another way not to be counterfeit is to be pure in heart.

<u>Prayer</u>

Dear Father,

Forgive me for not living a life that is comparable to that of the bee. I pray in the name of your son Jesus Christ that as of now, by your spirit, I will work to build up the body of Christ, and I will fulfil the assignment which you have given to me before the foundation of the world.

Help me, mighty God, to stay persistent in the task that you have given me and help me to be pure in my heart towards your work. Holy God, I cannot do it by myself, but I pray that your holy spirit will continue to lead and to direct my path in Jesus's name I pray. Amen

***

Chapter 2: The Analysis of Restoration

To the lost son as outlined in Luke 15

Jesus continued: "There was a man who had two sons. ¹² The younger one said to his father, Father, give me my share of the estate. So he divided his property between them.

¹³ Not long after that, the younger son got together all he had, set off for a distant country, and there squandered his wealth in wild living.

¹⁴ After he had spent everything, there was a severe famine in that whole country, and he began to be in need.

¹⁵ So he went and hired himself out to a citizen of that country, who sent him to his fields to feed pigs.

¹⁶ He longed to fill his stomach with the pods that the pigs were eating, but no one gave him anything.

¹⁷ When he came to his senses, he said, How many of my father's hired servants have food to spare, and here I am starving to death!

¹⁸ I will set out and go back to my father and say to him: Father, I have sinned against heaven and you.

[19] I am no longer worthy to be called your son; make me like one of your hired servants.

[20] So he got up and went to his father. But while he was still a long way off, his father saw him and was filled with compassion for him; he ran to his son, threw his arms around him, and kissed him.

[21] The son said to him, Father, I have sinned against heaven and you. I am no longer worthy to be called your son.

[22] But the father said to his servants, Quick! Bring the best robe and put it on him. Put a ring on his finger and sandals on his feet.

[23] Bring the fattened calf and kill it. Let's have a feast and celebrate.

[24] For this son of mine was dead and is alive again; he was lost and is found. So they began to celebrate." (Luke 15:11-24).

Introduction

You might be asking the question, is restoration in Christ necessary? But I want to tell you that it is necessary because restoration puts lifestyle change into a bigger picture than just preventing disease, feeling, and looking better or living longer. It also provides access to a God who heals and saves. But what is restoration? The Merriam-Webster dictionary defines the verb "restore" as to bring back to or put back something to a former or original state. Restoration is a repeated theme throughout the Bible, offering hope when all else seems to contradict it. From Genesis to Revelation, the Bible is filled with rich images of healing and restoration; it is a consistent and persistent theme in both the Old and New Testaments.

This theme of restoration provides a foundation for correctly understanding sin and suffering, God's plan for His creation, and his unstoppable quest to save His people and restore them to His image. It is the third of three parables in that chapter directed at a mixed audience of tax collectors, sinners, Pharisees (religious leaders), and teachers of the law. All three parables are on the topic of lost things being found: a lost sheep, a lost coin, and a lost son. Likewise, all three parables point to the heavenly joy over every sinner who repents from sin and turns to Jesus. Jesus had his specific audience, a mixture of "sinners" and "righteous," in mind when he told these three stories. Jesus was prompted to tell these parables because the Pharisees and teachers of the law were accusing him of welcoming sinners and eating with them (verse 2). The Pharisees and teachers of the law viewed themselves as righteous and the other half of the audience as sinners. Jesus told the stories of the lost sheep, coin, and son to clear up the matter of who is truly "lost".

The analysis of the concept of Restoration to the lost son as outlined in Luke 15 will give us hope of God's love and to put this virtue into practice.

The need for Restoration

There was a Need for Restoration as outlined in **Luke 15:13-16.**
Luke 15:14 says *"After he had spent everything, there was a severe
famine in that whole country, and he began to be in need".*

One can be restored when one recognizes that he/she needs help.
Verse 17 said *"When he came to his senses, he said, how many of
my father's hired servants have food to spare, and here I am
starving to death!"* There are some people out there that need help
and before they ask anyone for help, they rather die needing help, and
so it is because of pride why that person doesn't ask for help. Because
they care about what other people are going to say or think about
them. But you see, the prodigal son did not care at the time what
people would say about him, but rather he remembered what the
servants were eating in his father's palace and what they would have
left over and so he said that I will return to my fathers, because he has
a need and only his father can help him.

Everyone goes through a season at some point in their life but
when that season comes, make sure that you are on the right side of
the fence. The prodigal son was on the wrong side of the fence when
the season of drought reached him and so he was trying to fix the
situation by getting a job to feed the pigs, but with some situations
only Jesus can deliver you out of it. When you are on the right side of
the fence, Jesus said that **he can keep you from falling and present
you faultless**, and so if you find yourself on the wrong side of the

fence, return to Jesus and ask for help as David said **he is our present help in times of trouble**.

One can be restored when one admits that he/she is wrong. Verse 18 says **"I will set out and go back to my father and say to him: Father, I have sinned against heaven and you"**. For one to be restored one should admit that he is wrong. When Jesus was teaching his disciples to pray, he used the phrase **"forgive me of my trespasses"**, the word trespass means that *"you enter someone's land or property without permission."* And so, the prodigal son said that I will go back to my father and said I have sinned against heaven and you and so, he was restored. He recognized that he did not just sin against his father, but also against heaven and he knew that what he did was out of the will of God and not just out of the will of God but also out of the will of his father.

His portion of goods was always going to be there, but his timing was wrong. Likewise, as a Christian, there is a set timing for your blessing and if you are not mature enough to handle it, you can trip over it and your blessing become a stumbling block because you don't know how to handle it. It is very significant that the bible referred to the prodigal son as the younger of them. Sometimes we believe that we are ready for battle when we have never gone through any training and thereby take on the battle and believe we are all powerful and all mighty.

I remember in my early stage of walking with the Lord, how I was hungered for Jesus and hungered for his power. I remember seeing some people gambling in the community, and I did not consult God about the matter but rather, I took the matter in my hand and begin to pray about witchcraft and all manner of evil on the top of my voice and I begin to bind the devil and evil principalities. After finish praying, I went into my house and all of a sudden, I find myself on the bathroom floor so weak and I called my dad to come and help me up. He did not know what was happening to me, but I knew and so I started to pray and asked God to have mercy on me. And that is where I realized that I had taken matters into my own hands but then I heard the voice say *"the battle is not yours, it is the Lord's"*. I say that to tell you that God will bless you and because of immaturity, you can trip over your blessing because you believe that's all you want. And so it is today, where many of us want the blessing but don't want the one that blesses us. We can admit that we are wrong to him just like the prodigal son and he will receive us just like his father accepted him.

The Plea for Restoration

There was a Plea for Restoration as outlined in **Luke 15:18-19.** **Luke 15:19** says *"I am no longer worthy to be called your son; make me like one of your hired servants".*

One should plead to be restored because restoration put us in the plans of God. **Jeremiah 29:11** said, *"For I know the plans I have for you, declares the Lord, plans to prosper you and not to harm you,* *plans to give you hope and a future".* The prodigal son realized that only his father could have help him because his father even had plans for his servants where they even had bread to spare. Similarly, God has a plan for all of us and at times we are the ones who turn away from God, and so, we must go through the entire process again so that we can become the image that God has in his mind.

God sent Jeremiah down to the potter's house and while he was there, he saw the potter doing work on the clay but he said that the clay marred in the hand of the potter. In other words, it meant that the clay had its way or simply that it was deformed in the hands of the potter and the potter started the process all over again in a manner that pleased the potter. Likewise, with the prodigal son, he realized that he had turned away from the plan of his father and so he returned to him to ask him for mercy. The son did not mind even if his father made him into a servant, but because of the love that his father had for him, his father restored him in his rightful place. If you know that you are out of the will of God, like the prodigal son, I'm here to tell you that you can plea with God because **his mercy endures forever** and he will restore you to your rightful place in His kingdom.

One should plead to be restored because restoration will make us secure in God. **Proverbs 3:26** says *"For the Lord is your security. He will keep your foot from being caught in a trap".* When you are restored, you will no longer lean on your understanding but in your ways, you are going to acknowledge God and he is going to direct your path. The prodigal son didn't want to lean on his understanding anymore, but he needed security, which is his father, not just to fight for him but to provide for him. I'm here to tell you that God is a provider and he said that if you *"seek ye first the kingdom of God and his righteousness then all other things shall be added to you".*

One of the natures of God is to provide for his people. Another one of his natures is to take care of his people and also to fight for his people. But when the prodigal son left under his father's coverage, he moved from under his father's security and so the father would want to provide but could not be found. And so he realized that he must go back to his father, to get the security the servants were getting. And so brethren, we must plead with God so that he can restore us and give us his divine coverage.

The result of the Restoration

The Result of Restoration is outlined in **Luke 15:22-24. Luke 15:22 says** *"But the father said to his servants, Quick! Bring the best robe and put it on him. Put a ring on his finger and sandals on his feet".*

Restoration is always in abundance. Verse 22 says *"But the father said to his servants, Quick! Bring the best robe and put it on him. Put a ring on his finger and sandals on his feet".* When God is restoring you, it is always in abundance. When the prodigal son returned to his father and repented, the father said to his servants bring forth the best robe and put it on him, put ring on his finger, shoes on his feet and not only that but bring also the fatted calf. Before the prodigal son left his father's house, he might not have been wearing the best robe, or ring on his finger, or shoes on his feet but when he returned, he did not just receive any robe but he received the best.

There was something that everyone in the father's house has their eyes on and probable hoping one day they can receive it, and that's the fatted calf because after he has received the fatted calf, there was a problem. When God restores you, at times it causes problem even with your brothers and sisters, and all of a sudden they remember your past and want to paint your past on your face but I have news for them, the songwriter says *"if anybody asks you just who I am tell them that I am redeemed"*.

You have some preachers out there that might have sinned in their past and up to this day, persons believe that they cannot be restored but let God be their Judge. Likewise with the prodigal son, his big brother said in verse 30 ***"but as soon as this thy son was come, which hath devoured thy living with harlots, thou hast killed for him the fatted calf"***. Thank Jesus that God is not like man and so one should seek God to be restored because restoration is always in abundance.

Restoration brings happiness. Verse 24 says **"For this son of mine was dead and is alive again; he was lost and is found",** so, they began to celebrate. When you are restored, there will be joy and happiness. And so, when the prodigal son had been restored in his father's house, the bible says that they began to celebrate. And if by any chance, you have been lost and the cares of this life burden you down, you can turn to Jesus because in him there is joy and in him, there is pleasure. The bible says when one person in Christ has repented, the angels in heaven rejoice. The bible also says that **in his presence there is fullness of joy and at his right hand there are pleasures forever more**. It is time for us to turn like the prodigal son and return to our father's house.

<u>Summary</u>

Therefore, having analyzed the concept of Restoration as outlined in Luke 15, we should be mindful of the love of God and practice it. There was a Need for Restoration as outlined in **Luke 15:13-16**, and one can be restored when one recognizes that he/she needs help, and one can be restored when one admits where he/she went wrong.

There was a Plea for Restoration as outlined in **Luke 15:18-19**, and one should plead to be restored because restoration put us in the plan of God. One should also plead to be restored because restoration will make us secure in God. The result of Restoration as outlined in **Luke 15:22-24** shows us that Restoration is always in abundance, and Restoration brings happiness.

Prayer

Dear Father,

I want to thank you for the love that you have shown toward me. Thank you for not leaving me or forsaking me. I want to thank you for forgiveness because without forgiveness where would we be today. Even when I have acted immaturely, yet your love towards me is great. Thank you Lord for your grace and your mercies, help me God to overcome the spirit of pride so that I will not stay in my situation and die but rather give me the spirit of humility, that when I am wrong, I will admit that I am wrong and cry out for your mercies. Thank you, Lord, for restoring me when I cry out to you and I pray that you will allow your holy spirit to lead and guide me so that I will not move out of my time. In Jesus's mighty name I pray. Amen

***

Chapter 3: Putting Your Faith in Jesus

5 "When Jesus had entered Capernaum, a centurion came to him, asking for help.

6 Lord, he said, my servant lies at home paralyzed, suffering terribly.

7 Jesus said to him, Shall I come and heal him?

8 The centurion replied, Lord, I do not deserve to have you come under my roof. But just say the word, and my servant will be healed.

9 For I am a man under authority, with soldiers under me. I tell this one, Go, and he goes; and that one, Come, and he comes. I say to my servant, Do this, and he does it.

10 When Jesus heard this, he was amazed and said to those following him, Truly I tell you, I have not found anyone in Israel with such great faith.

11 I say to you that many will come from the east and the west and will take their places at the feast with Abraham, Isaac, and Jacob in the kingdom of heaven.

12 But the subjects of the kingdom will be thrown outside, into the darkness, where there will be weeping and gnashing of teeth.

13 Then Jesus said to the centurion, Go! Let it be done just as you believed it would. And his servant was healed at that moment.

14 When Jesus came into Peter's house, he saw Peter's mother-in-law lying in bed with a fever.
15 He touched her hand, and the fever left her, and she got up and began to wait on him.

16 When evening came, many who were demon-possessed were brought to him, and he drove out the spirits with a word and healed all the sick.

17 This was to fulfill what was spoken through the prophet Isaiah: He took up our infirmities and bore our diseases". **(Matthew 8:5-17)**

Introduction

Faith in Jesus will make you victorious in every aspect of your life. Based on what is happening around us and in our lives, you might be asking the question of why we should put our faith in Jesus. I want to tell you today that when you put your faith in Jesus, you will overcome every strategy of the enemy. But what is this faith? According to the bible in the book of **Hebrew Chapter 11:1, *"... faith is the substance of things hoped for, the evidence of things not seen".*** This is not so much a definition of faith but rather a declaration of what faith does. It is the substance of things that are hoped for. And the word substance there has been translated in a newer version of the Bible as substantiating the things that we hope for. And the evidence, that word has been translated as conviction of the things not seen. I'm convicted of truths, though I may not have seen them, I'm convicted of their existence. There is evidence for the existence of God, and it causes me to believe in God. Though I have never seen God, the evidence of His existence creates that faith in my heart.

I want to tell you that there are many things that we believe in that we don't and haven't seen. We believe in the wind, though we haven't seen the wind. We see the effects of the wind. We see the trees that are bowing in their force. We see the leaves that are blowing. We see the dust that is being carried. We see the evidence of it. You can feel it. We say, "Oh, that's a cold breeze, and you feel the wind. You see the evidence of it, and thus, we believe in the wind, though we don't see the wind itself.

Magnetic force, I believe in it, but I've never seen it. I see its effect as it brings opposite poles together and I watch them attract. And so, I believe in the magnetic powers or the magnetic force, but I have never seen it. I see evidence of it.

I see evidence of God. I feel the presence of God. I feel the power of God. I feel the love of God. And I see the evidence of God's existence, and thus, faith. I believe in the existence of God, though I've never seen God. Yet, I do not doubt His existence, because of the evidence that is all around. Faith is the substantiating of the things that are hoped for, the evidence of things not seen. For by faith, the centurion man went to Jesus knowing that his servant will be healed by his word.

This centurion was a heathen, a Roman soldier. Though he was a soldier, he was a godly man. He did not allow his calling or will placement to be an excuse for ungodliness. Even though he was a commander of soldiers, he did not allow his earthly authority to stop him from going to Jesus.

Every Christian must put their faith in Jesus.

We are going to look at three reasons why one should put their faith in Jesus. One should put their faith in Jesus because:

I.   Faith in Jesus Brings Healing.

Verse 13 says *"Then Jesus said to the Centurion, Go! It will be done just as you believed it would"* and his servant was healed at that very hour.

1.   Healing comes when you go to Jesus in Humility. Verse 5 says **"the Centurion came to him asking for help"**.

The centurion came to Christ with humility. He was a man of power and authority but came on behalf of his servant for Christ to heal him. Christ's word alone heals man. Christ, who is our maker and redeemer, will save us but we must come to him in humility. It may not always be in the way we want but he gives us what we need for our salvation.

Just as a parent doesn't always give their children what they want but gives them what they need, Christ does the same. We are children of God, and the reality is we do not know what we need or want. But God knows what we need, and he gives it to us when we call upon him. But do we receive whatever he gives us with gratitude and joy, including trials and difficulties, or do we get upset and angry? This brings me back to the book of Job. While Job was going through his calamities he did not get upset and angry but rather he said in **Job 1:21** ***"Naked I came from my mother's womb, and naked I will depart. The LORD gave and the LORD has taken away; may the name of the LORD be praised".***

I want to tell you that when you praise God in your situation, it confuses the enemy. And so, for this centurion, Christ healed his servant because it was what was needed for his salvation at that time. We may not always get physical healing, even the Apostle Paul dealt with physical torments and pains but as he said, it was for his salvation and so that he would not boast and in his weakness, God's grace was made known and strong. Just as the centurion came to Christ in humility, we must come to Christ with humility and an open heart so that he can grant us salvation.

2. Healing also comes from the spoken word. Verse 8 said, ***"But just say the word, and my servant will be healed".***

The Centurion understands the power of the spoken word from a ruler's standpoint, so basically he was telling Jesus, I know that you are a man that is under the authority and I know that you can speak and things happen, because ***"I am a man under authority with soldiers under me, where I tell this on go he goes and that one comes and he comes".*** But even though he has authority over his soldiers yet he could not speak to his servant to be healed and so he must put his faith in another ruler to speak for him which is Jesus Christ.

Some of us may put our trust in Palm Readers and Astrologers but even they too need divine interventions. As believers, we must understand that the battle is not ours but the Lord's. David said to Goliath, I come against you in the name of the LORD Almighty. We must understand that when we speak, we don't speak what we want but we speak his will, as Paul tells us that ***it is no longer I who live but Christ that lives in me.***

I want to tell you my friends that you are under a higher authority which is Jesus Christ, and you too have authority and power here on the earth. It has been said from the beginning, ***"let us make man in our image and likeness and let them have dominion over all the earth".*** The bible calls us peculiar people, a royal priesthood. So you too can speak and things happen for **greater is he that is in you than he that is in the world**.

One should put their faith in Jesus because:

II.   Faith in Jesus Brings Deliverance.

Verse 16 says *"When evening came, many who were demon-possessed were brought to him, and he drove out the spirits with a word"*.

1. Deliverance will come when you know him to be a deliverer. Verse 6 says *"my servant lies at home paralyzed, suffering terribly"*.

The Centurion understands that Jesus is a deliverer and knows that he has authority over sickness and diseases, and so he said to Jesus, just speak the word and my servant shall be healed. I want to say to you my colleague that when you know Jesus to be a deliverer, in times of sickness and obstacles, he will remove it, in times of demons possession he will overpower them, in times of trials and temptations he overcomes, in time of persecutions he strengthens, in times of bounds in chains he breaks chains, and in time of bondage of sin, he will set us free.

Jesus delivered Paul and Silas out of prison in Philippi. I want you to picture the scene. It was midnight in the dungeon. The two missionaries, bound with chains, were *"praying and singing hymns to God"* when God used an earthquake to break the chains and open the doors. Through this dramatic event, God saved an entire family and brought glory to Himself. You don't have to be locked in physical bonds to be suffering in bondage. There are many kinds of "chains" that fill this life. You have emotional chains, mental chains, and spiritual chains. But no bond is so strong that Jesus cannot break it. And so, Paul and Silas replied and said, ***"Believe in the Lord Jesus, and you will be saved, you and your household".*** **(Acts 16:31)**

2. Deliverance will come when you allow him to dwell in your house. Verse 14 says ***"When Jesus came into Peter's house, he saw Peter's mother-in-law lying in bed with a fever".***

For Jesus to dwell in your house you must first accept him in your house, he said in **Rev 3:20** ***"Behold, I stand at the door, and knock: if any man hears my voice, and open the door, I will come unto him".*** And so, by accepting him in your house is to make Christ live in your heart as the Apostle Paul said ***"So that Christ may dwell in your hearts through faith. And I pray that you, being rooted and established in love, may have power, together with all the Lord's holy people"*** and to make Christ live in your heart is to allow his Kingdom to reign over you as the angel said to Mary in the book of **Luke 1:33,** ***"and he will reign over Jacob's descendants forever; his kingdom will never end".***

For His Kingdom to reign over us is for his will to be done in our lives and no more we will pray our will but for his will to be done. For his will to be done in our life is for us to walk by faith and not by sight.

Just as Peter allowed Jesus to come into his house, we should also allow him into our house.

One should put their faith in Jesus because:

III. Faith in Jesus Secure your Place in the Kingdom of God.

Verse 11 says *"I say to you that many will come from the east and the west and will take their places at the feast with Abraham, Isaac, and Jacob in the kingdom of heaven"*.

1. You can secure your place in heaven when you understand the authority of the Kingdom. Verse 9 says *"For I am a man under authority".*

For one to understand the authority of the Kingdom, you must know the authority you are under, and so the Centurion man knew the authority he was under, but the authority that he was under could not heal his servant. The authority that he was under has a certain limit and so he could only operate physically. He understood that Jesus not only operates physically but also spiritually.

The Bible says in **John 3:2** that Nicodemus went to Jesus by night and said to him, *"we know that you are a teacher who has come from God. For no one could perform the signs you are doing if God were not with you."* I want to tell you, my friend, that when you know the authority, you are under *"No weapon that is formed against you shall prosper, and every tongue that shall rise against* *you in judgment thou shalt be condemned".* When you know the authority you are under, Jesus will anoint you for his will and it's the anointing that breaks every yoke of the devil as David said *"thou anoints my head with oil; my cup runneth over".*

You can only understand the authority of the kingdom when you know what is written in the law of the kingdom and the law of the Kingdom is the word of God. Paul the Apostle says in **2 Timothy 3:16-17,** *"All Scripture is given by inspiration of God, and is profitable for doctrine, for reproof, for correction, for instruction in righteousness, that the man of God may be complete, thoroughly equipped for every good work".* The book of **Psalms 119:89** says *"Forever, O LORD, your word is settled in heaven".* The Word of God is the only source of absolute divine authority. This divine authority is for you and me as servants of Jesus Christ.

2. You can secure your place in heaven when you exercise the authority of the kingdom. Verse 9 says *"For I am a man under authority, with soldiers under me. I tell this one, 'Go,' and he goes; and that one, 'Come,' and he comes. I say to my servant, 'Do this,' and he does it".*

As believers of the Kingdom of God, it has been expected that we exercise the authority of that kingdom. **Jeremiah 1:10** says *"See, I have this day set thee over the nations and the Kingdoms, to root out, and to pull down, and to destroy, and to throw down, to*

build, and to plant". When you put your faith in Jesus like that Centurion man that believes that if Jesus only speaks the word his servant will be healed, I want to tell you that the word is already spoken, he says in **Jeremiah 29:11** that *"for I know what I have planned for you, says the LORD. I have plans to prosper you, not to harm you. I have plans to give you a future filled with hope".* I want to tell you that when you exercise the authority of the kingdom, it cancels every storm of the enemy. In verse 23 of Matthew 8, while Jesus and his disciples entered the ship, a great tempest arose in the sea so much that the waves covered the ship and the disciple went to Jesus saying "thou carest that we perish", but Jesus said "O ye of little faith", and so, I believed that Jesus wanted them to understand that they too can speak to the winds and the waves by faith. I want to tell you my friends that you have the authority and power to cancel every activity of the devil in the name of Jesus. Many of us might be under the bondage of Satan but I tell you that if you exercise the authority of the Kingdom, you will be delivered, and so I beseech you to exercise that authority in Jesus' name.

<u>Summary</u>

Therefore, let us put our faith in Jesus because faith in Jesus will bring you healing, and this healing will come when you go to Jesus in humility, and this healing will come when you believe in the spoken word. Let us put our faith in Jesus because faith in Jesus will bring you deliverance, and deliverance will come when you know him to be a deliverer, and deliverance will come when you allow Him to dwell in your house. Let us put our faith in Jesus because faith in Jesus will secure your place in heaven, and you can secure your place in heaven when you understand the authority of the Kingdom, and you can secure your place in heaven when you exercise Kingdom authority.

<u>Prayer</u>

Our father, who is in heaven, I want you to help me not to be shaky where my faith in you is concerned. Help me God to overcome the spirit of doubt because if I doubt that you heal, then how will I receive my healing? If I doubt that you deliver, then how will I get my deliverance?

Lord, help me to believe because it is in my nature to have faith and I want to thank you for your Kingdom authority which you have given us before the foundation of the world. Thank you for your strength and your might in Jesus name. Amen.

***

Chapter 4: God's Solution to the Problem of Divorce

[24] *"Now as the church submits to Christ, so also wives should submit to their husbands in everything.*

[25] *Husbands, love your wives, just as Christ loved the church and gave himself up for her*

[26] *to make her holy, cleansing her by the washing with water through the word,*

[27] *and to present her to himself as a radiant church, without stain or wrinkle or any other blemish, but holy and blameless.*

[28] *In this same way, husbands ought to love their wives as their bodies. He who loves his wife loves himself.*

[29] *After all, no one ever hated their own body, but they feed and care for their body, just as Christ does the church -*

[30] *for we are members of his body.*

[31] *For this reason, a man will leave his father and mother and be united to his wife, and the two will become one flesh.*

[32] *This is a profound mystery - but I am talking about Christ and the church.*

[33] However, each one of you also must love his wife as he loves himself, and the wife must respect her husband. **(Ephesian 5:24-33).**

Introduction

Divorce should never be a choice in any marriage. It has been said that *"divorce is the process of terminating a marriage or marital union. Divorce usually entails the cancelling or reorganizing of the legal duties and responsibilities of marriage, thus dissolving the bonds of matrimony between a married couple under the rule of law of the country or state".* There are a lot of responsibilities within marriages, hence with divorce, we must reorganize our duties and as time passes, we will realize that divorce leads to unhealthy changes within the union. And so, this problem is evident within our churches and homes, and there has been a constant seeking for a cure for the problem. And so, there is…

I. The need for a solution to the problem of Divorce

1. **The increase in divorce is allowing younger couples to shy away from the holy covenant.**

But what is this saying to you? It is saying that there will be a decrease in marriages and an increase in fornication and adultery. A lot of young people are finding marriage unattractive because they observe their own parents' marriages and they do not like what they see. They don't see them being happy, they hear them complain and they see the quarrels. They see marriages as a way of being trapped and getting out of it can be expensive. But why would I want to enter something that will not make me happy? Why would I want to enter something that could cost me my life? These are the thought of our future generation. And so, many have divorced because people are getting married for the wrong purposes. Some people marry for romance, but then the romance dies, while others see marriage as a contract; that means I have something that you need. But that should never be any reason for marriage, thus there is a need for a solution to the problem of divorce.

2. According to The Gleaner, the number of persons applying for divorce in the year 2020 was 3,689, while in the year 2021, 4,381 applications were submitted.

And so, that is showing us that as the years are passing, divorce is growing in numbers. We are living in an age when divorce is readily accessible, where spouses are quickly opting for separation rather than working to save their relationships. People separate sometimes even by failing to communicate properly, and one of the common things you will hear is that 'he doesn't know how to talk to me or 'whenever I'm talking to him, he goes silent,''.

And so, I want to tell you that in today's world, people are getting divorced for the simplest of matters and it is pushing the younger generation away from even thinking about marriage. I was watching an interview the other day and the topic was about marriage and the young lady said that she doesn't want to get married because 'marriage is bondage'. She continued to say after seeing what another married couple went through; she said she doesn't want to be a part of that. And so, if we can fix the mindset of married couples or even those that are entering into marriage, then I believe it will paint a brighter picture of the holy union.

3. **The judgment of divorce ends the marriage and spells out the specifics about how the couple will allocate custodial responsibility and parenting time, child, and spousal support, and how the couple will divide assets and debts.**

People generally don't get married assuming they'll eventually divorce. Though divorce is common, you might feel perfectly confident that your marriage will last. Divorce, much like a marriage, tends to be a life-altering event. The process alone can bring plenty of changes, from quieter meals to an empty house, or even a new house. If you have children, your co-parenting schedule could mean spending days without them for the first time. As you begin to adjust to the altered shape of your life, you might experience a complex blend of thoughts and feelings ranging from betrayal and loss to anger, or even relief. To put it simply, divorce can throw your life into turmoil. And so, as you begin to re-establish yourself, you should keep in mind that divorce doesn't mean your life has ended. Rather, it signals a new beginning.

But what are some of the solutions that experts find to fix the problem of divorce...

II. Extra-Biblical Solution to the Problem of Divorced

1. Remain faithful. Dr. Finnegan Alford-Cooper studied 576 couples who had been married for 50 years or more; in 1998, she released her findings in the book For Keeps: *Marriages that Last a Lifetime.* In her study, she found that 95 percent of the spouses agreed that fidelity was essential to a successful marriage, and 94 percent agreed or strongly agreed that marriage is a long-term commitment to one person. While a whopping 90 percent of the couples she surveyed said that they were happily married after 50-plus years.

Sylvia Smith, an Expert Blogger puts the word faithfulness into three categories: 1) fulfilling his/her duties and obligations, 2) being trustworthy, and 3) being loyal to your spouse. Smith said that when we get married to a person, one of the things that we would include in our vows is how we would be able to take care of them, to do our best so we can fulfill our duties and responsibilities as their spouse. This doesn't just end in providing financially for our family. It includes loving, sharing life, and most importantly respecting that person. She said "Being trustworthy with the littlest promises to the biggest tests of fidelity is something that everyone should be ready for. Aside from being loyal to your vows, you, as a married person, shall no longer try to commit to another relationship and should resist any temptation that you will encounter. Another solution is to…

2. Be friends with your partner. John Gottman—a psychology professor who claims his research will predict with 91 percent accuracy, whether a couple will stay together, says the key to marital happiness and success is friendship. Some of the most important aspects of this type of friendship are knowing each other intimately, demonstrating affection and respect for each other daily, and genuinely enjoying each other's company. Gottman based his findings on 25 years of marital research, which he presented in his book *The Seven Principles for Making Marriage Work*. Gottman says Friendship between couples means they "know each other intimately" and "are well versed in each other's likes, dislikes, personality quirks, hopes, and dreams," Gottman believes the principles that make a marriage work are "surprisingly simple."

First, happily married couples aren't smarter or more beautiful than others, and they don't live in castles in the clouds where there are no conflict or negative feelings. They've simply learned to let their positive feelings about each other override their negative ones. They understand, honour, and respect each other. They know each other deeply and enjoy being together. They do little things every day to stay connected and to show each other they care. In short, they are friends. And so, happy marriages are based on a foundation of friendship. Another solution is to…

3. Say "I love you" every day. This is especially important when you're not feeling the sensation of love; at these times, you must actively generate it. Saying those three little words, and performing loving gestures, will warm both your and your spouse's hearts. According to Dr. Donald Johnson, he said a woman experiences mood swings. This experience often causes changes in behaviour. She could be laughing at this moment and in a few hours, she is as serious as a judge.

This is due to a biological change that the woman goes through. Johnson said as she goes through her monthly cycle several biological changes take place. Firstly, she experiences premenstrual tension. This affects her body system and influences her emotions and behaviour. Secondly, the red blood cells in the woman's body are less than that of a man. Because these red cells are responsible for conveying oxygen to the different parts of the body, less oxygen capacity tends to affect the body mechanism of the woman thereby influencing her moods and feelings.

What is God's Solution to the Problem of Divorce?

III.   The Biblical Solution to the Problem of Divorce

1. Love your Wife. Ephesians 5:25 *"Husbands, love your wives, just as Christ loved the church and gave himself up for her".* The key word here is 'Love'. Love is a word commonly used by everyone in our society, but sometimes we don't seem to understand this word. But can we love someone and beat them, belittle them, criticize them, or even sometimes kill them? This couldn't be love. A definition of love is *"the ability to look beyond the fault of the individual and to respect and appreciate the person."* It can also be defined as those unreserved feelings that keep people or family together in good times and in bad times.

Love is therefore accepting, appreciating, and wanting an individual to feel good. It is a bond or connection between two people that results in trust, intimacy, and interdependence that enhances both partners. I can't help but think about Jesus, you see, Jesus loves us without measure, he loves us with compassion, mercy, and respect. His love is pure, constant, and passionate to us, no matter how imperfect we are. If a man doesn't love his wife in that same way, he will abuse his authority and his headship and as a result, will abuse her. Because you and your wife become one, you must treat her the way you would treat your own body. Would you do anything to deliberately hurt or destroy your body? No, because you love your body and care for it. Take a moment to analyze what you do for your body and how you feel about it. You provide physical care for your body throughout the day. Much of your happiness is dependent upon the health of your body.

The Apostle Paul says in verse 33 of **Ephesian 5** *"let each one of you in particular so love his wife as himself"*. A man should never withhold love from his wife. Doing so, you will lose her in one way or another. The wise man Solomon also states, in the book of **Proverbs Chapter 3:27** *"Do not withhold good from those to whom it is due when it is in the power of your hand to do so"*. A man should therefore ask God to increase his love for his wife and ask God to enable him to show it in a way that makes her beautiful. Another Biblical solution is that...

2. The wife should submit to her husband. Ephesian 5:24 said, *"Now as the church submits to Christ, so also wives should submit to their husbands in everything"*. Many out there believe that submission is a sign of weakness, but I'm here to tell you that submission in marriage is a sign of strength, not of weakness. It requires a great degree of personal strength of character. Submission in marriage is a spirit of respect a wife has toward her husband. It is an attitude intended to help her and her husband to live a more content, peaceful life together.

Problems and disagreements between a husband and wife in marriage are inevitable. But when a woman has an attitude of submission in marriage, and a heart of respect for her husband, it is much more likely the inevitable problems will be resolved harmoniously, without unpleasant quarrelling, and without bitterness and resentment. And that is not to say it will be so because the man dominates and gets his way all the time. Some people look down on submission as if it were something demeaning, degrading, or humiliating.

In a biblical sense, that is not what submission in marriage is about. For a wife practicing submission to her husband does not mean she should be a silent "yes" person or doormat. Nor does it mean she should have no opinions of her own. Rather, a wife who chooses to take an attitude of submission towards her husband is a wife who has a heart of being supportive of her husband. She does so because she chooses to. In choosing to support her husband, she is empowering him to have the self-respect he needs.

He will develop into the kind of man who accepts his role and responsibilities in the home. He will seek to carry out his God-ordained position of protecting, providing for, and leading his family. When a wife submits, she is being a helper to her husband in the broad, biblical sense of that word. That is what God was referring to in **Genesis 2:18**, God said, ***"It is not good for the man to be alone; I will make him a helper suitable for him"***. When a wife submits to her husband, it is not because she is afraid of his reproof, domination, rejection, or chastisement. Instead, it is because she chooses to bless him. In so doing, she is demonstrating a spirit of respect for men.

The blessings of such an attitude and actions in turn elevate her in the eyes of her husband. Additionally, this brings contentment and satisfaction to the couple and the marriage. For a husband, when his wife demonstrates a heart of submission in marriage, she is a pleasure to be around. The husband finds appreciation and admiration for her because she is one whom he can trust. As a result, he can feel at peace and content. He can trust her with his deepest desires and fears because he is not afraid of her scorning him, competing with him, or rejecting him. He can relax with her because he knows that even when he makes mistakes, she will be working with him to help him put them right. The husband can feel secure in himself that she will be working to minimize the consequences of his mistake rather than trying to prove a point or reject him in some way. A man whose wife truly understands, and practices biblical submission acquires a greater sense of self-respect. He knows she respects him as a husband who accepts his responsibility as a leader in the home. He has confidence that she respects him, and she is not in any way trying to belittle him.

Summary

Therefore, when we are confronted with the problem of divorce, we should give heed to God's solution as outlined in **Ephesians 5:24-33**, where the wife should submit to her husband and the husband should love his wife.

<u>Prayer</u>

Dear God,

I want to give you thanks for the love that you have shown towards me. Help me Lord to take heed to your solution about divorce because I cannot do it by myself, but with you Lord, I can do all things through Christ who gives me the strength. Be glorified, mighty God and be praised, in Jesus name. Amen

***

Chapter 5: The Importance of Love

To Spiritual Formation based on 1 Corinthian 13

[1] *"If I speak in the tongue of men or angels but do not have love, I am only a resounding gong or a clanging cymbal.*

[2] *If I have the gift of prophecy and can fathom all mysteries and all knowledge, and if I have a faith that can move mountains but does not have love, I am nothing.*

[3] *If I give all I possess to the poor and give over my body to hardship that I may boast, but do not have love, I gain nothing.*

[4] *Love is patient, love is kind. It does not envy, it does not boast, it is not proud.*

[5] *It does not dishonour others, it is not self-seeking, it is not easily angered and, it keeps no record of wrongs.*

[6] *Love does not delight in evil but rejoices with the truth.*

[7] *It always protects, always trusts, those hopes, always persevere.*

[8] *Love never fails. But where there are prophecies, they will cease; where there are tongues, they will be stilled; where there is knowledge, it will pass away.*

[9] *For we know in part and we prophesy in part,*

[10] but when completeness comes, what is in part disappears.

[11] When I was a child, I talked like a child, I thought like a child, I reasoned like a child. When I became a man, I put the ways of childhood behind me.

[12] For now we see only a reflection as in a mirror; then we shall see face to face. Now I know in part; then I shall know fully, even as I am fully known.

[13] And now these three remain faith, hope, and love. But the greatest of these is love. (1 Corinthians 13).

Introduction

It has been said that **1 Corinthians 13** is classified as "the hymn of love" in the New Testament as it is one of the books with the most discussions of love. It also shows a relationship with chapter 12 in which Paul addresses people's spiritual gifts while in chapter 13, he hopes to drown out the Corinthians mounted level of competitiveness that they hold with one another.

The Corinthians are pondering on whose spiritual gifts are greater and better than others to establish some sort of superiority, and so in chapter 13, Paul leads them to focus on their motives and questions them by saying to them that they need to love one another, and not just one another, but they should love everyone else as well because we are all children of God.

This chapter addresses the connection of our spiritual gifts with the love of God and our relationship with Him. These actions of love in Chapter 13 are a representation of the presence of God Himself. And so, Love as described in 1 Corinthians 13 is best understood as a way of life, lived in imitation of Jesus Christ, that is focused not on oneself but the "other" and his or her good.

Paul declares love as the greatest power in a community that seems to be lacking in a lot of it. This moment is a far cry from an adoring couple standing at the altar declaring unwavering devotion to each other. The members of the Corinthian church, to whom chapter 13 is directed, are nowhere near a love fest.

The Countercultural Love

In the previous verse (12:31) the intention of Paul was not to make this to be random aside from the definition of love, but rather he is saying this because love is what makes spiritual gifts meaningful. And so, countercultural has been the description of Paul by the action and behaviour produced by love. It talks contrary to envy, pride, and self-centeredness to the Christians in Corinth which also speaks to our current generation.

We are living in a time where we are more of "self" rather than living for each other, and so to present a way in which a person lives for others would be highly provocative. Christ must remain the example. In Paul's description of love, he gives no space for love to be less than serving others.

The gifts of the Spirit, as useful as they were for the assembled people, were meaningless when executed for individual glory or greedy dreams. Paul's depiction of the role of love begins by his mentioning two constructive qualities: patience and kindness. Paul follows that by comparing love to negative qualities; he contends that love is not **"envious or boastful or arrogant or rude. It does not insist on its way; it is not irritable or resentful"** (1Corinthians 13:4-5). In the end, Paul states positively that love **"rejoices in the truth. It bears all things, believes all things, hopes all things, endures all things"** (1Corinthians 13:6-7).

Paul makes it clear that love begins when someone else's need supersedes one's own. The envy, boasting, rudeness, arrogance, and anger of normal life will be turned upside down. Instead, patience and love and rejoicing in truth are to mark out God's people. In line with the way Christ forgave our sin and no longer holds it against us, our love is to hold no record of evil.

Many believers have failed to handle when a person sins against them, and even though they said that they forgive, the hurt or pain remains in the back of their minds. And when another person did them wrong, they remembered and kept on scoring. And so, the nature of a Christian is to forgive and to forget, because when one forgives then that person will gradually forget.

In the book of Micah, chapter 7, verse 19, the prophet said that ***"God would cast our sins into the deepest sea"*** and so as believers, that should be our nature. We are reminded of Peter's question about how often to forgive his brother when he sins against him **(Matthew 18:21)**. The answer Jesus gives is that life must be lived as a forgiving life. Disciples of Christ will go on and on forgiving because it is part of who they are. Love is the most excellent way. *(ZA Blog, 2011), (First Baptist Church, 2021), (Society of Biblical Literature, 2022).*

Love is Not Soft

It is believed by many that love is an attitude of 'niceness'. This means that any dispute, or any firm tone over important matters, and any strong spiritual discipline or disciplining of another is to be regarded as unloving. And so, in some churches, this has even led to the dilution of the Christian faith being preached with little emphasis on holiness, lest some should feel condemned or unloved.

In **2 Timothy 4:3-4**, Paul wrote of the risks of letting the world's understanding of situations like this influence the church. He said, ***"For the time is coming when people will not endure sound teaching but having itching ears, they will accumulate for themselves teachers to suit their passions and will turn away from listening to the truth and wander off into myths"*** **(ESV) (ZA Blog, 2011).**

A modern myth is that love will tolerate all things, promote all things, and deny nothing. The Bible defines love beautifully for us where God is love, and the perfect demonstration of that love was shown by Jesus to all of us. In this chapter, Paul goes further down to earth about love when he said in **1 Corinthians 13:6** that ***"It does not rejoice at evil"*** and so certainly, love is not soft. It will always seek to build up the other, but that does not mean turning a blind eye to sin or not calling out evil in another person.

True love is supremely seen in the gospel of Jesus Christ and will often separate people and so this is what happens when the gospel has been preached and lived out. While Paul can urge patience and insist on kindness when he says ***"Love is patient, love is kind"***, he sees no contradiction between this and possibly bringing a "rod" to the Corinthian church. In **1 Corinthians 4:21**, he writes: ***"Shall I come to you with a rod of discipline, or shall I come in love and with a gentle spirit?"*** Neither does he see a conflict between God's love and God's severe discipline of his people; **Hebrews 12:6**, for example, tells us that ***"the Lord disciplines the one he loves"***. It is critical when presenting the love inherent in the gospel of Jesus Christ that it is not reduced to meaningless platitudes and the "smiley face" of yesteryear. Love is not soft *(ZA Blog, 2011)*.

Christ-like Love

Love is a way of thinking, acting, living, and a way of being as a person, in other words being Christ-like. And so, Paul's letter to the Corinthians shows what this looks like in his own life in the ninth chapter. He said to them that *"Though I am free and belong to no one, I have made myself a slave to everyone, to win as many as possible. To the Jews I became like a Jew, to win the Jews. To those under the law, I became like one under the law (though I am not under the law), to win those under the law. To those not having the law, I became like one not having the law (though I am not free from God's law but am under Christ's law), to win those not having the law. To the weak I became weak, to win the weak. I have become all things to all people so that by all possible means I might save some. I do all this for the sake of the gospel that I may share in its blessings"*.

Love in its completest and most extensive meaning is the true love to God and man, a compassionate personality of the mind towards our fellow Christians, growing out of sincere and fervent dedication to God. He also tells them that they should imitate him (Paul). The idea of "love," in contrast with "knowledge" and grace gifts, is introduced earlier in the letter, in **1 Corinthians 8:** *"We know that we all possess knowledge, but knowledge puffs up while love builds up"*. The argument in 8:1 that "love builds up" reminds the reader that when Paul speaks of "building up" the church or the body, he thinks of love in action in the community. The focus of love here is thus predominantly the believer or the church, the understood object of "to build up" *(ZA Blog, 2011), (Bible Study Tools, 2022)*.

Love is the key

In his love poem, Paul makes a decisive shift, diminishing the allure of spiritual gifts and functions. Tongues, prophecy, knowledge, miracles, and servanthood to the point of death are important, but they still do not qualify as the *"more excellent way"* **(1 Corinthians 12:31)**. Love is the key. Because of the popularity of **1 Corinthians 13** in our modern context, it is easy to miss the flexibility Paul exercises concerning the triad of faith, hope, and love **(1 Corinthians 13:13)**.

Most people think Paul's list is fixed with faith first, love as the bookend, and hope as the middle. Paul uses this triad elsewhere and in a different configuration. He tailors the triad to fit the community he addresses. For example, in the Letter of **1 Thessalonians**, the triad appears twice, in both instances, the order Paul rehearses is faith, love, and hope **(1 Thessalonians 1:3; 5:8)**. Paul shifts the order because the Thessalonian church exceled in faith and love, but struggled with hope **(1 Thessalonians 1:8; 3:6)**, especially hope for the future **(1 Thessalonians 2:19, 4:13)** *(Luther Seminary, 2020)*.

Accordingly, Paul underscores the importance of love in **1 Corinthians 13** because it is the spiritual resource the Corinthians want most. Paul describes "the work of love" in both encouraging and bad terms. On the encouraging side, Paul says love is patient, kind, and selfless. It involves truth-telling, courage, constancy, and tolerance **(1 Corinthians 13:4-5,7)**.

In terms of what love "is not," Paul says it is not self-seeking, short-tempered, and offensive. In other words, love does not harm individuals. It does not damage expectations for genuine community. Love does not hinder the encouragement of another's humanity. Love is the only means by which followers have a chance to live fully in the understanding and fellowship of God. All other spiritual gifts and human accomplishments provide restricted entry to that reality **(1 Corinthians 13:8-12)**.

Make no mistake. The love Paul is talking about here is not passive and fluffy. This kind of love is an up at dawn, feet on the land, tools in hand, working kind of love. It builds communities. It develops positive social connections, and not just social networks (which many of us have come to prefer). Paul's declaration of love unifies. Love is the way by which we talk to each other **(1 Corinthians 1:5; 16:20)**, eat with one another **(1 Corinthians 8:13; 10:27; 11:33-34)**, communion together **(1 Corinthians 11:20)**, and affirm all **(1 Corinthians 16:15-16, 18)**.

Love surpasses our self-imposed status systems and personal preferences. It forms whole and holistic people, who are secure in the well-being of others. Love will not let us down if we truly live in it together **(1 Corinthians 16:14)** *(Luther Seminary, 2020)*.

Misconception of Love

Paul exposes the folly of the misguided Corinthian Christians: they were taking pleasure in entirely temporary things. Will there be prophecy in heaven? Of course not! (Why not?) Will there be tongues in heaven? Will there be faith or hope in heaven? No! There will be no need for any of that! For example: what should we treat with greater honour: honour jewellery or an heirloom diamond? The diamond, of course, because it is of greater importance and greater solidity. That's exactly what Paul is saying about spiritual gifts and love. Which of those things will last forever? Love. That's the value.

Now, we only see some of "the big picture", but when we are with God, we will finally be complete and know everything that we could ever know. Paul is saying that the Corinthian Christians were behaving like children. They had no perception, they were being childish, and they had no sense of true value and significance. And so, love is not about one's feeling or emotion, but rather an action which should characterize all relationships between the children of God.

And so, 1 Corinthians would be a great passage to memorize for marriages, parents, church members, and all relationships. And so, if one could embrace this love realistically and responsibly as Paul intends, there would be a revolution in our lives, in our families, and churches *(First Baptist Church, 2021)*.

The Practical Application of Love

A good context of love is to practice pursuing the needs of others before looking at yourself. At the forefront of Paul's mind, was the application of this kind of love happening in the daily communications with the Corinthians in the church gathering, and relationship to twitches outside. And so, it gives meaning to the character of God and therefore should also give us meaning. This love will inform all relationships a Christian has in the church, at home, at work, and play. Paul even echoes this sentiment in **(Philippians 2:1-11)** where he calls on the church to do nothing out of selfish motivation but instead humbly consider others before oneself. In **1 Corinthians 13:1-13**, Paul was addressing the use of gifts when the church assembled. This chapter falls between chapters 12 and 14, where Paul addresses "the gifts of the Spirit."

The personal expression of gifts or abilities had created interpersonal tensions in the church body, and the Corinthian followers had begun to personalize worship at the cost of the corporate grouping. They were fascinated with glossolalia, the Spirit's gift of "speaking in tongues" (speaking in dialects unknown to the assembly. Paul recognizes the usefulness of the gifts in the opening verses starting with the tongues, prophecy and ending with giving to the poor, but he is quick to note that when done without love they are empty. Paul hoped to prove that the Corinthian church (which was full of separation and strife) could change and be a substantially better place if members chose the path of love *(Society of Biblical Literature, 2022).*

The Transforming Love

When you think about transformation, the best example in all of nature is the butterfly. The butterfly undergoes a transformation when it emerges from the cocoon that it had woven for itself when it was a caterpillar. When this love invades our lives, we are similarly transformed. We are changed from the inside out. It starts with a changed heart.

When we allow God to transform us with his love, he changes our hearts. He removes all the sin, all the self-seeking, all the guilt, all the self-loathing. We become captivated first in our hearts by his great love. Then he begins to work on our minds. He changes the way we think about things and people. He enables us to love unconditionally just as he loves! Our attitudes change. Compassion and forgiveness replace judgmentalism and retribution. When our attitudes and thoughts change our actions follow close behind *(Wolstenholm, 2022).*

Paul states in **1 Corinthians (13:4-8)** that *"Love is patient, love is kind, it does not envy, it does not boast, it is not proud. It does not dishonour others, it is not self-seeking, it is not easily angered, and it keeps no record of wrongs. Love does not delight in evil but rejoices with the truth. It always protects, always* *trusts, hopes, and always perseveres. Love never fails".* And so, a major theme of 1 Corinthians, therefore, is the transforming power of Christ's love for the individual and the church. Paul wrote about the love that is put into practice. More than just a feeling or emotion, Paul writes less about what love *is* and more about what love does.

Transformed by the love of Jesus Christ, this kind of love should be a natural overflow of the believer's heart and evident in everything they do. The words used in **1 Corinthian 13** to describe love are the kind of active verbs Paul was challenging the Corinthian church to adopt: patience, kindness, humility, forgiveness, trust, hope, and perseverance. Love, Paul argued, was the greatest outward testimony of their inward transformation.

At the beginning of **1 Corinthians 13**, Paul writes, *"If I speak in the tongues of men or angels, but do not have love, I am only a resounding gong or a clanging cymbal"* **(1 Corinthians 13:1)**. He then goes on to say that if Christians can prophesy, can understand the mysteries of the universe, and give to the poor but ultimately lack love, their actions are meaningless, and there is no spiritual gain. Love must be at the root of everything Christians do and evident in their actions. This is in alignment with the teachings of Jesus, who said, *"By this everyone will know that you are my disciples, if you love one another"* **(John 13:35)**.

Summary

Therefore, love is what makes spiritual gifts meaningful, and so countercultural has been the description of Paul by the action and behaviour produced by love. And so he shows that it is a lot more than an attitude of 'niceness' and that there will come a time when people will not endure sound teaching, but having itching ears, they will accumulate for themselves teachers to suit their passions and will turn away from listening to the truth and wander off into myths.

And so, love does not rejoice at evil and certainly, love is not soft. Love is a way of thinking, acting, living, and a way of being as a person, in other words, being Christ-like. Paul says love is patient, kind, and selfless. It involves truth-telling, courage, constancy, and tolerance **(1 Corinthians 13:4-5,7)**. And so, love is more than a feeling or an emotion, but must include actions that should characterize all relationships between the children of God. This love will inform all relationships a Christian has in the church, at home, at work, and at play and if we put this love into practice, we will be transformed into the image that God desires.

<u>Prayer</u>

Dear Lord,

I want to thank you for the love that you have shown toward me. I pray that your love will be seen within me so that my spiritual gift can be meaningful and complete. Help me Lord to put your love into practice so that I can be transformed into your image and your likeness. Thank you for dying for me even when I did not deserve you but because of your love, you have sent your only begotten son to die for me. Thank you Lord. In Jesus's name. Amen

***

Chapter 6: Increase in Faith

By Studying the Mustard Seed

"He replied, "Because you have so little faith. Truly I tell you, if you have faith as small as a mustard seed, you can say to this mountain, Move from here to there, and it will move. Nothing will be impossible for you". (Matthew 17: 20)

Introduction

When looking at the foundations of the Christian life, some principles include prayer and worship, but the key one is faith. Putting our trust in God, that He will take care of the future and provide for all our needs. Jesus spoke about the power of faith several times in his teachings and used multiple metaphors to explain what faith is and how important it is, but I believe one of the most powerful metaphors is that faith can be like a mustard seed. The truth about any seed is that it does not remain a seed.

Seeds contain an embryo, which is a group of cells ready to form roots, a stem, and the first leaves. Once the coat around the seed is moistened, the embryo cells expand and burst out into a process called germination. First, the roots will develop and push out and down into the soil to make sure the new plant can get water. Then the stem cells stretch up to display the first leaves. The embryo uses food stored in the seed to power its initial growth until the leaves can start producing food.

Small seeds like the mustard don't have much-stored food, so they must fall in just the right spot to be successful and therefore grow into a full-sized plant. But the mustard trees are huge, despite the size of their seeds. The seed is the smallest of all seeds in the world. With the exact size of around 1 to 2 millimetres, it is an important herb that is being used in many regional foods.

For a first-century farmer, a variant of mustard seed which is known as the black mustard seed was the smallest seed that they have ever sown. They grow best in hot and dry climates. From this tiny seed, a tree can grow up to 20 feet tall and 20 feet wide. The mustard tree has roots that dig deep into the ground which allows the tree to grow in some of the harshest environments. Its roots allow it to flourish in times of drought and rocky places. From January through to April, the tree produces 2- to 5-inch-long panicles of small, greenish-yellow flowers. After pollination, those flowers set pea-size fruits that ripen to a maroon shade; each fruit contains a single seed.

Although sweeter than the leaves, the fruits also have a pungent flavour and can be consumed raw, dried, or cooked. A mustard tree is also called toothbrush tree because the tender young sticks cut from the tree has been used as an antibacterial tooth cleaner for hundreds of years. People wishing to "brush" their teeth generally strip off a young stick's bark and chew on the stick's inner fibres. Those fibres provide the peelu often found in alternative toothpaste. Growing mustard trees from seeds begin with soaking a mustard tree's fruits in lukewarm water for one to three days until their pulp has been reduced to a runny texture. Strain the pulp through fine cheesecloth to collect the tiny, brown seeds.

While they are still moist, scatter the seeds in a seedling flat or other container filled with damp sand, and press them into the sand's surface. If their pulp which contains germination **inhibitors** has been completely removed, the seeds should begin to sprout within 24 hours. Keep the container on a heat mat so the sand's temperature stays in the mid-80s to mid-90s Fahrenheit to produce the best results. Mustard trees grow slowly.

The study of the mustard seed in **Matthew 17: 20** will help the believers to increase their faith in God.

Seek to Grow in Christ

As the mustard trees grow huge, despite the size of their seeds, as Christian we should also seek to grow in Christ.

1. The mustard seed is one of the smallest seeds in the world, yet the tree can grow up to the size of about 20 feet tall and 20 feet wide. And its leaves are an important herb that has been used in many regional foods. Likewise, as children of God, even though our faith in God might not be huge but there is a possibility that our faith in Jesus

can reach a place in Jesus like that of the Centurion man, which said to Jesus that I am not worthy to have you come under my roof but rather speak the word and my servant shall be healed. And Jesus' response was, I have never seen such great faith in all Israel.

I want to tell you that faith begins where the will of God is known, and we must go out and find it. In the book of **Hebrew 11:16**, it says *that "without faith, it is impossible to please God, because anyone who comes to him must believe that he exists and that he rewards those who diligently seek him".* Let me tell you my brother and sisters that you can find great faith in any Kingdom like that of the Centurion man who was a man of authority, and Power which tells us that he was of a Kingdom. Brothers and sisters, we are all a part of the Kingdom of God, as it was spoken from the beginning when God said, "let us make man in our image and our likeness and let them have dominion over all the earth." But because of sin, the bridge between God and man was broken and we were signed out of the Kingdom of God, but with the blood of Jesus Christ, the bridge was now mended and we now have a connection with the Kingdom of God but to receive back that great faith, we have to sign into the Kingdom and that is why Jesus tells us that we should *seek ye first the Kingdom of God and his righteousness and all other things shall be added unto you.* Brethren, we must seek God's Kingdom to operate in the great faith of the Kingdom.

2. Growing a mustard tree begins with soaking a mustard seed in lukewarm water for one to three days until its pulp has been reduced to a runny texture. In comparison to the children of God, we should soak ourselves in the presence of Almighty God so that he can transform us into the image and likeness of God our saviour. Because without God in our life, nothing is worthwhile. Without the presence of Almighty God in our life, we have no strength, no substance, and no stamina but with him, everything will have meaning, purpose, and effectiveness.

The songwriter says, *"In Your presence, that's where I belong, In Your presence that's where I am strong, seeking Your face, touching Your grace, in the cleft of the Rock, in Your presence oh God"*. Some of us might believe that we can only find joy and happiness in this world but **Psalm 16:11** said that **"in his presence is fullness of joy; at His right hand there are pleasures for evermore".** And so, it is our duty as believers to stay in the presence of Almighty God, because our faith increases when we stay in his presence. Breakthroughs will come, change will begin to take place when we stay in his presence, deliverance will come, when we stay in the presence of Almighty God, we will not walk in the lust and pride of this world.

Rooted and Grounded in God

As the roots allow the mustard tree to flourish in times of drought and rocky places, regarding Christians, we should be rooted and grounded in God.

1. The mustard tree will survive in every season because the root of the tree is deeply planted and will go wherever the water is underground. Likewise as children of God, it is our duty to be rooted and grounded in Christ so that when our season of drought comes, we will be able to stand firm and continue to bear fruit as **Jeremiah 17:8** said ***"For he shall be like a tree planted by the waters, which spreads out its roots by the river and will not fear when heat comes; But its leaf will be green, and will not be anxious in the year of drought, nor will cease from yielding fruit"***.

When we are rooted and grounded in Christ nothing can move or shake us out of place because we are connected to the source, we are connected to the true vine of life and no drought can stop us from bearing fruits because we are connected to the fountain of God. The hymn writer says *" There is a fountain filled with blood drawn from Immanuel's veins; and sinners, plunged beneath that flood, lose all their guilty stains"*. I hear a lot of people are saying that a time is coming when there will be no food on the earth because the trees are going to stop bearing, but you see the bible tells me in **Genesis 8:22** that ***"As long as the earth endures, seedtime and harvest, cold and heat, summer, and winter, day and night shall never cease"***. And I made that point to let you know that as long as we are connected to the stream of life, our leaves shall never be withered and we will continue to bear fruit in every season. So let us remain rooted and grounded in Christ.

2. At times the root will meet upon rocks along the path, while going down in search of water, but the root will never stop at the rock but rather wrap itself around the rock until it finds water. As believers no matter what is before us, we should not take our eyes off Jesus and set our affection upon him. You see when our eyes are set upon Jesus, no matter what is before us, it cannot shift us because Jesus is the source of our lives, and if we keep on looking at Jesus, like the root of the mustard tree which is in search of water, then we cannot **stop,** we must be persistent and determined.

There is believer out there that is dry because they are not connected to the source of life, you see, the water is the source of life for the growth of the mustard tree and so as believers we have to stay connected to Jesus for us to grow spiritually. For without Jesus, there can be no growth, there can be no life, you see all thing are possible with him, and without him nothing is possible. And so, it is our responsibility to search for him and stay connected to him because he is the way, the truth, and the life.

Take our Time to Grow

As the mustard tree takes its time to grow slowly, as believers, we should also take our time to grow in God, *study to show thyself approved*.

1. The mustard seed will germinate slowly when it is planted in the soil at a temperature below 40 degrees, and so for the seed to

germinate, it must wait until the soil warms up. As children of God, the more we study and apply the word of God to our life, that is how our faith starts to increase. Brothers and sisters for our faith to grow in God, it simply means we need to grow spiritually. This is to mature in both knowledges of God and in a godly living, to conclude, it is to become more like Christ.

Just as a person grows physically from an infant to a mature adult, a Christian's life is designed to grow spiritually from baby to mature Christian. **1 Peter 2:2-3** said that, ***"Like new born infants, long for the pure spiritual milk, that by it you may grow up into salvation if indeed you have tasted that the Lord is good".*** But then you have a set of believers that believe that they are in church long enough and so you who are seeking growth in the holy spirit can't say anything to them, but it is not how long you are in a church that gives you spiritual growth, but rather how much of Christ you have become.

But by right, they should have grown but for some reason or another, they are still at the baby stage and so **Hebrews 5:12-13** speaks against believers who had failed to grow in faith: ***"For though by this time you ought to be teachers, you need someone to teach you again the basic principles of the oracles of God. You need milk, not solid food, for everyone who lives on milk is unskilled in the word of righteousness, since he is a child".*** To grow in faith involves growing in God's Word and its application. Paul also used similar words to condemn some of the practices of Christians in

Corinth: *"But I, brothers, could not address you as spiritual people, but as people of the flesh, as infants in Christ. I fed you with milk, not solid food, for you were not ready for it. And even now you are not yet ready, for you are still of the flesh. For while there is jealousy and strife among you, are you not of the flesh and behaving only in a human way?"* **(1 Corinthians 3:1-3).** Paul notes that he began with feeding them "milk" or with spiritual basics. Yet they were still not ready for solid food, as their maturity was lacking.

<u>Summary</u>

Therefore, having seen the increase in faith as shown in the study of the mustard seed, as believers we should be able to develop a life that is comparable to that of the mustard seed. As the mustard trees grow huge, despite the size of their seeds, as Christians, we should also seek to grow in Christ no matter how small our faith is.

There is a possibility that our faith in Jesus can reach a place in Jesus like that of the Centurion man and we should also soak ourselves in the presence of God so that he can transform us in the image of God. As the roots allow the mustard tree to flourish in times of drought and rocky places, likewise, as children of God, we should be rooted and grounded in Christ and so it is our duty to be rooted and grounded in Christ, and no matter what is before us, we should not take our eyes off Jesus and set our affection upon him.

As the mustard tree takes its time to grow slowly, as believers, we should also take our time to grow in the grace and knowledge of Jesus Christ, and the more we study and apply the word of God to our life, that is how our faith starts to increase.

<u>Prayer</u>

Our Father, who art in heaven, hallowed be thy name, your kingdom come, and your will be done in my life as in heaven. Lord, I want to thank you for the many times your grace and your mercy overshadows me, many times Lord, I have walked in doubt and fear but I pray today that my life will now be a shadow of that of the mustard seed where I will seek to grow in you no matter how small my faith is, so that I can be transformed in the image of Christ. In Jesus name I pray. Amen

***

Chapter 7: God's Divine Protection

Whoever dwells in the shelter of the Highest will rest in the shadow of the Almighty.

² I will say of the Lord, "He is my refuge and my fortress, my God, in whom I trust."

³ Surely, he will save you from the fowler's snare and the deadly pestilence.

⁴ He will cover you with his feathers, and under his wings, you will find refuge; his faithfulness will be your shield and rampart.

⁵ You will not fear the terror of night, nor the arrow that flies by day,

⁶ nor the pestilence that stalks in the darkness, nor the plague that destroys at midday.

⁷ A thousand may fall at your side, ten thousand at your right hand, but it will not come near you.

⁸ You will only observe with your eyes and see the punishment of the wicked.

⁹ If you say, "The Lord is my refuge," and you make the Highest your dwelling,

¹⁰ no harm will overtake you, no disaster will come near your tent.

¹¹ For he will command his angels concerning you to guard you in all your ways;

¹² they will lift you in their hands so that you will not strike your foot against a stone.

¹³ You will tread on the lion and the cobra; you will trample the great lion and the serpent.

¹⁴ "Because he loves me," says the Lord, "I will rescue him; I will protect him, for he acknowledges my name.

¹⁵ He will call on me, and I will answer him; I will be with him in trouble, I will deliver him and honor him.

¹⁶ With long life I will satisfy him and show him my salvation." (Psalms 91).

Introduction

God's protection will give us his divine coverage. There are a lot of things that are happening around us and in our lives that you may be asking the question, does God protect His people? But I want to tell you that when you **stay under God**, He will **stay over you.** But what is this Divine Protection? According to Sanjeev Patra *"**Divine** protection, in its true and real sense, means the soul's welfare so that nothing can* *bring harm to it or be an obstacle to its happy growth and divine fulfilment."* Another definition said that *it is the act of supernaturally shielding someone from harm, injury, or danger.* It is God's way of defending or shielding man from every form of evil; it is supreme and dependable. Divine protection is your covenant right if you are born again; it is one of the packages of redemption in Christ and so many Commentaries say that the Psalm has no title, and therefore the author remains unknown. Because it shares some of the themes of Psalms 90, some think Moses was the author. Because it shares some of the themes and phrases of Psalms 27, and 31, some think the author was David. Some of its language, of strongholds and shields, reminds us of David, to whom the Septuagint ascribes it; other phrases echo the Song of Moses in Deuteronomy 32, as did Psalms 90; but whether it is written by David or Moses it is saying one thing, that God protects his people.

Every believer should stay under God's protection to be safe.

We are going to look at three results why one should stay under God's protection. The first result for one staying under God's protection is that:

God's protection will keep us Steady

God's Protection will keep us Steady, verse 11 says **"For he shall give his angels charge over thee, to keep thee in all thy ways"**.

1. God will keep us steady when we put our trust in him. Verse 2 says **"He is my refuge and my fortress: my God; in him will I trust".** When we put our trust in God as believers, no storm of this life can move us. When we put our trust in God, we can join the songwriter and sing *"I shall not, I shall not be moved, just like the tree planted by the waters, I shall not be moved".* When we put our trust in God my brethren we can say like the prophet Isaiah that **"No weapon formed against us shall not prosper, and every tongue which rises against us in judgment it shall be condemned".** But trusting in God is never always easy, but who says that this road is going to be easy, I can hear the songwriter that said, *"it is a hard road to travel and a mighty long way to go........"*

The bible says that the road that leads to eternal life is straight and narrow, but one thing is for sure, if you waiver not while trusting in Jesus, it will be worth it after all, as the songwriter say *"After all this life is over and my burdens have been lifted and I stand upon the mountain top so tall, looking over to that city that the saviour is preparing, gives me faith that I can make it after all".* Brothers and sisters, we need to put our trust in God because we have no other help but Almighty God.

2. God will keep us steady when we live in His presence. Verse 1 says **"He that dwelleth in the secret place of the highest shall abide under the shadow of the Almighty".** When you live in God's presence, it is like building your house out of bricks on a rock. I remember a story about the three little pigs that decided that they were

going to build their houses, the first little pig built his house out of straw, the second little pig built his house with sticks and the third little pig built his house with bricks. But then a wolf came out of the woods, and he huffed and puffed and blew the first little pig's house down and likewise the second but when he reached the third house that was made out of brick he huffed and puffed but nothing happened, and he repeats huffing and puffing until he was tired.

I want to tell you that when you live in the presence of God no matter how the devil huffs and puffs, he can never move you because it is no longer you who lives but Christ that lives within you.

The Second result for one staying under God's protection is that:

God's Protection will keep us Safe

God's Protection will keep us Safe- verse 3 says **"Surely, he shall deliver thee from the snare of the fowler, and the noisome pestilence"**.

1. God will keep us safe from the plans of the enemy. Verse 3 said **"Surely, he shall deliver thee from the snare of the fowler"**. The enemy is always plotting against us as believers, but God is always ahead of the enemy protecting us and so the psalmist said surely, he shall deliver thee from the snare of the fowler. The plan of the enemy has never changed, and that plan is to steal, kill, and destroy. The devil wants to steal your joy and give you sorrow, he wants to kill your anointing and give you lukewarmness, he wants to destroy your mind

and control it. But Jesus said I came that you may have life and have it more abundantly.

I'm here to tell you that this is the day that the Lord has made, let us rejoice and be glad in it. One of the major fights that we get as believers is in our prayer life because prayer reveals the trap of the enemy, and so the enemy doesn't like a believer that prays, but the bible encourages us that men always ought to pray and not faint. My friends, the devil is always planning and so it is up to us to stay connected to God by prayer so that God can deliver us from the plans of the enemy.

2. God will also keep us safe from plagues. Verse 10 says ***"Neither shall any plague come nigh thy dwelling"***. God will allow his angels to protect his children from the attacks of the adversary, seen and unseen. As we look into the book of **Exodus 12** verse 23, we see where the death angel was passing through to kill all the firstborn sons of the Egyptians but for the ones that the Lord wanted to stay alive, the blood was used as a sign of protection from the death angel, and so when we obey the instruction of the Lord, no affliction can come upon us as children of God.

And so, I can't help but think about Jesus, that while we were yet sinners, Christ died for us and so death cannot take us out when he wants us because the blood of Jesus still flows. The songwriter says, *"still it flows, still, it flows as fresh as ever, still, it flows as fresh as ever from thy saviour wounded side"* Even amid the Coronavirus, we can see where the

Lord has protected us from this plaque and even if it reached us, it couldn't take us out because the devil cannot take us out without God's permission. You see, it is like the devil to destroy God's people but as long as we are under God's protection, he has to ask for permission. In **Job 2**, the devil asks God for permission to touch his servant Job…

The result for one staying under God's protection is that:

God's Protection will keep us Satisfied

God's protection will keep us satisfied. Verse 16 says "With long life will I satisfy him".

1. God will satisfy us when we call upon Him. Verse 15 says "He shall call upon me, and I will answer him." When we as believers call upon the name of the Lord, indeed we will be satisfied because only God can truly give us that satisfaction. David cried out in **Psalms 121** and said *"I will lift my eyes unto the hills from whence cometh my help, my help comes from the Lord who makes the heavens and the earth".* This was a prayer from the depths of David's heart as he cried out to God knowing that God is his ultimate source in every situation of his life. He knew that when he called upon the name of Jesus, demons and devils have to back up, situation changed in the atmosphere and chains are broken at the mention of the name of Jesus. **Philippians 2** verse 10 says *at the name of Jesus every knee*

shall bow and every tongue shall confess that Jesus Christ is Lord.

We will be satisfied with God because we know that he is the one who holds our future and not man, you see, you have some persons that believe that if I don't use you then you can't be used, but when God is ready, you have moved. The songwriter says *"you got to, you got to move when God gets ready you got to move."* God will never leave you nor forsake you, which means that he is ever-present with us even when we think he is so far away from us. Jesus said I will send you a comforter that will lead you into all truth. What assurance and joy it is to know that our heavenly father loves us that much and in all this, we will find peace.

2. God will satisfy us with His Salvation. Verse 16 says **"With long life will I satisfy him and show him my salvation".** No one can be satisfied without Jesus, no matter the number of riches you have. **Mark 8:36** said **"For what will it profit a man if he gains the whole world, and loses his soul?"** Some persons may think that riches are all they need to be satisfied. The devil said to Jesus **"turn these stones into bread"** but Jesus said that **"man shall not live by bread alone but by every word that proceeds out of the mouth of God".** A big house won't satisfy you, your account filled with money won't satisfy you, in all of that, you still need Jesus.

The hymn writer said, *"there is no satisfaction without salvation"*. I want to tell you that the pleasures of this life cannot satisfy you, but find pleasure in Jesus. The Bible said that in his presence there is fullness of joy and at his right hand there are pleasures forever more. The psalmist says that the Lord wants to satisfy you with long life, but we need to cry out to him. Let us look to him today.

Summary

Therefore, let us stay under God's protection because God's protection will keep us steady, and He will keep us steady when we trust in Him. He will also keep us steady when we live in his presence.

Let us stay under God's protection because God's protection will keep us safe, and He will keep us safe from the plans of the enemy. He will keep us safe from every plague.

Let us stay under God's protection because God's protection will keep us satisfied, and He will satisfy us when we call upon Him, and He will satisfy us with His salvation.

<u>Prayer</u>

Dear Lord,

I want to thank you for your protection, thank you for keeping me safe from every trap of the enemy. I pray that through the Holy Spirit, you will continue to satisfy my soul with your salvation, in Jesus's name. Amen

***

<u>Conclusion</u>

Therefore, having seen the nature of kingdom workers as shown in the study of the nature of the honeybees, we as Christians should be able to develop a life that is comparable to that of the bees. As the honeybees work to make their colony happier and more productive, as Christians, we should be workers also to build the body of Christ, and we can build the body of Christ by loving our neighbour, and we can build the body of Christ by fulfilling our assignment.

As honeybees are optimistic, as Christians we should also be optimistic, and we can be optimistic by focusing on the positive, and we can be optimistic by staying persistent. As honeybees are not counterfeit, as Christians we should not be counterfeit Christians, and one way not to be counterfeit is to follow Jesus, and another way not to be counterfeit is to be pure in heart.

The concept of Restoration is outlined in Luke 15. We should be mindful of the love of God and practice it. There was a Need for Restoration as outlined in Luke 15:13-16, and one can be restored when one recognizes that he/she needs help, and one can be restored when one admits where he/she went wrong. There was a Plea for Restoration as outlined in luke15:18-19, and one should plead to be restored because restoration put us in the plan of God, and one should plead to be restored because restoration will make us secure in God.

The result of Restoration as outlined in Luke 15:22-24 shows us that Restoration is always in abundance, and Restoration brings happiness.

Let us put our faith in Jesus because faith in Jesus will bring you healing, and this healing will come when you go to Jesus in humility, and this healing will come when you believe in the spoken word. Let us put our faith in Jesus because faith in Jesus will bring you deliverance, and deliverance will come when you know him to be a deliverer, and deliverance will come when you allow Him to dwell in your house. Let us put our faith in Jesus because faith in Jesus will secure your place in heaven, and you can secure your place in heaven when you understand the authority of the Kingdom, and you can secure your place in heaven when you exercise Kingdom authority.

When we are confronted with the problem of divorce, we should give heed to God's solution as outlined in Ephesians 5:24-33, where the wife should submit to her husband and the husband should love his wife.

Love is what makes spiritual gifts meaningful, and so countercultural has been the description of Paul by the action and behaviour produced by love, and so he shows us that it is a lot more than an attitude of 'niceness' and that there will come a time when people will not endure sound teaching, but having itching ears they will accumulate for themselves teachers to suit their passions and will turn away from listening to the truth and wander off into myths. And so, "love does not rejoice at evil" and certainly, love is not soft. Love is a way of thinking, acting, living, and a way of being as a person, in other words being Christ-like. Paul says love is patient, kind, and selfless. It involves truth-telling, courage, constancy, and tolerance (1 Corinthians 13:4-5,7). And so, love is more than a feeling or an emotion but must include actions that should characterize all relationships between the children of God. This love will inform all relationships a Christian has in the church, at home, at work, and at play and if we put this love into practice, we will be transformed into the image that God desires.

The increase in faith is shown in the study of the mustard seed. As believers, we should be able to develop a life that is comparable to that of the mustard seed. As the mustard trees grow huge, despite the size of their seeds as Christian we should also seek to grow in Christ no matter how small our faith is and there is a possibility that our faith in Jesus can reach a place in Jesus like that of the Centurion man. We should also soak ourselves in the presence of God so that he can transform us in the image of God.

As the roots allow the mustard tree to flourish in times of drought and rocky places, likewise as children of God, we should be rooted and grounded in Christ and no matter what is before us we should not take our eyes off Jesus and set our affection upon him. As the mustard tree takes its time to grow slowly, as believers, we should also take our time to grow in the grace and knowledge of Jesus Christ, and the more we study and apply the word of God to our life, that is how our faith starts to increase.

Let us stay under God's protection because God's protection will keep us steady, and He will keep us steady when we trust in Him. He will keep us steady when we live in his presence.

Let us stay under God's protection because God's protection will keep us safe, and He will keep us safe from the plans of the enemy. He will keep us safe from every plague.

Let us stay under God's protection because God's protection will keep us satisfied, and He will satisfy us when we call upon Him, and He will satisfy us with His salvation.

Reference

1. Gottman, John, *The Seven Principles for Making Marriage Work,* (1999)

2. Cooper, Finnegan, *Marriage that Lasts a Lifetime,* (1998).

3. Johnson, Donald, *how to choose your soul mate and build a marital Relationship.*

4. New International Version (NIV) (1984)

5. https://zondervanacademic.com/blog/1-corinthians-131

6. https://www.workingpreacher.org/commentaries/narrative-lectionary/faith-hope-and-love/commentary-on-1-corinthians-131-13

7. https://www.fbcthomson.org/post/understanding-love-from-1-corinthians-13

8. https://www.bibleodyssey.org/en/passages/main-articles/love-passage

Made in the USA
Middletown, DE
07 April 2023

28402842R00059